The Fly
Volcano

Eule Grey

love from
Eule
pp

All Luce wants is to go home, but how can she? Since the war, her beloved city has been under an enchantment. Rivers run dry and the streets are haunted, or so they say.

When she hears a rumor that the curse has been lifted, Luce writes a heartfelt letter to the leaders. It begins ten years ago, when she's thirteen-years-old and dying of a broken heart. Dying, I tell you!

Luce's account takes the leaders into the cold heart of a mermaid. To when she, and her bestie, Adu, live in a spidery, clifftop house with a tiny dog.

Not even Sea Mother's magic or mermaids can hold back the war. When the world goes dark, it takes a wind magician and the strongest love of all to save her family and friends.

Light up the skies, little mermaid!

Can be read as part of the Volcano Chronicles series or as a stand-alone.

Warnings: Weapon use, conflict, and crisis.

This story depicts children and young adults in situation of war.

The Curse of Sea Mother

Sea Mother, she's the ocean
The dams and winding river
Take not her babes,
Ignore their says,
Or all in Craw shall wither.

1

Dear Craw Advisory Board,

I'll keep the introduction and credentials brief. My name is Luce. I'm the daughter of Arker Fi, the mermaid artist. I was born in central Craw and fled ten years ago, on the day the bomb exploded. I haven't returned. How could we, when the city's frozen in time by Sea Mother's curse?

I'm sure you know our history as well as I. No rivers or waterfalls will flow into Craw. Not a drop. Crops and plants don't flourish. Houses collapse. They say soldiers guard the gates and the streets are riddled with diseases... That's all we know.

In my opinion, the curse is fair and just. Sea Mother warned you what would happen, but you didn't listen.

Why am I writing? Be patient, and I'll get to it. You might say a buzzing little bee is to blame. It sped through Mainland carrying a precious message. That gift was passed from person to person, and one day, it landed at my door.

Maybe you've also heard the rumour? *Craw is recovering.* I can hardly write without jumping up and down. Recovering, I tell you!

I didn't believe it at first, and neither did Ma. It was too wide a leap. We did what Crawians always do in times of trouble—turned to the sea for answers.

"What do you think, fish?"

There was no reply.

"Seals? Have you heard anything?"

It seems they hadn't. But the Fi family are rather stubborn and don't give up easily. Towards dusk, something blew in with the scuttling turtles. Ma heard it first, and then I did. It was the essence of a whisper; a promise from far away.

Sea Mother, she shall rise.

The rebirth of Craw? *She's* inviting us home? I'm not ashamed to say I cried. My city that fits like skin. I want it so much, so much. Home. *Home.* How difficult to write that word which wiggles and squirms like a bag of snakes. It'll never be still.

So anyway, advisors, I'll get to the purpose of this letter. It's about your precious advisory board. Who're the members? Leaders who fled, is it? Rich folk who donated money to weaponry manufacturers?

Shame on you. How dare you! What gives you the right to represent Craw without inviting—begging—Arker Fi to advise *you*? I'm sure I don't need to list my mother's achievements, but I will do, all the same.

Have you seen the mermaid statues that line the streets? And the town square that's protected by a hundred stone women, each with more majesty and dignity than you can imagine? *My mother* made those, as well as thousands of mermaid dolls. When the lights of Craw dimmed, what do you think those kids reached for? Your guess is correct—Ma's mermaids.

The last mayor named Arker Fi a forever guardian of Craw. In recognition of her work in schools and around the city. Because of her visionary art. No filthy war can delete such honor. A board of self-appointed advisors can't pretend it didn't happen. You know I'm right, cheapskate though you may be.

I ask you this: can a city be born without foundations? Can there be birth without a mother? You know the answer as well as I.

I'm moving too fast. Sorry. At least we both know where we stand.

Consider this letter an application for a role on your advisory board on behalf of my mother. I won't apologise for my boldness or beg for our rights. I never was much good with manners.

My account is a diary. It tells of the most powerful love—that of a thirteen-year-old girl. That was ten years ago. I'm twenty-three now, so I should know. If you don't like it, you can shove potatoes up your nose.

Oh, but we climbed inside the heart of a mermaid. The very heart, I tell you. It was colder than ice and as tough as a clam shell. I didn't think we'd survive. But then, nothing worth having is easy. You already know this. Afterwards, we were changed. The parts of us that were already strong grew as tough as mermaid pearls. The other parts? We don't talk about those.

This is my story.

2

I was born near Craw beach and grew up alongside seals, crabs, and turtles. Every creature that lived within the waters was my friend, including those who resided within our songs and legends.

The first time I saw a mermaid? I was thirteen, as I said. In a filthy mood and dying of a broken heart. Dying, I tell you.

Ten years ago, the fighting in the city became intolerable. Ma woke us in the middle of the night with the order to leave our home in Craw central. Right that instant. Leave now!

I didn't go easily. Would you? I was in the mood for a fight. "No way. What about saying goodbye to my friends?"

Ma disregarded my question without a thought. "No."

It seemed to me she didn't care, and it incensed me. "Can I leave our new address with Adu?"

"No," she said.

"Can I fetch my books?"

"Get in the car. It's time to leave," Ma said.

That's how it was. Unfair and unreasonable. Never one to do as told, I locked my bedroom door and swore at everyone. "Go away. Get lost."

It took Da, Granma, and Granda to talk me down from my tower of anger and entice me outside.

I stomped to the car, carrying a bag filled with my most treasured possessions but without my friends from the sea.

Everyone suffered from my bitter complaints. When Da offered me a drink, I refused. "From a cow's breast. Disgusting."

Though I grudgingly agreed to eat pastries for Granma's sake. Truthfully, I was tired and worried. When the engine started, I soon fell asleep with my head on Da's shoulder.

We woke to greyness and a spindly house moulded from wind and sea spray. I looked around in dismay and thought about running away.

"Where are we? I want to go home. Immediately," I said.

Ma spoke as fast as a flowing river. Much like I did when in trouble and ordered to the head teacher's room. "Just outside Craw. It won't be forever. You can get to the sea through the garden gate. It'll be all right."

The house was a fright. A fright, I tell you! Spidery and awful. The absolute worst thing—no Adu. I looked around the empty, whitewashed rooms, and realised I'd expected to find her there, waiting for me. Since babies, we've never been apart.

"I miss her already! What do you expect me to do? How can I have a fulfilled life without Adu? I'll *die* from the lack of her company. What girl can exist without her best friend?" I said, often. Especially when Ma was listening.

My mother ignored me.

Da laughed and took me down the broken path that led to the beach. "Come, come, Miss Doom. See the rock pools and seals? Notice one peeping up? He's come to say hello. And over there—beautiful sand flowers. You can bring paints and a canvas. It's not so bad."

"But why? *Why* are we here? The trouble is miles away. Craw's not at war. Not exactly," I said.

Though much of Mainland was, kindled by ancient jealousies and power-crazed leaders. The world changed when the Ansar and Skarle volcanoes blew, and refugees from two islands sought a place to live. Not every country treated them with compassion.

Ma says people grew greedy and hateful. Forgot our ancient lore that insists on togetherness and connectivity.

War raged across Mainland. We Crawians liked to think we were made of better stuff. Steps were taken to suppress fighting. Dividing walls to keep us apart, and soldiers positioned at every street corner. Times were hard, no doubt, but I firmly believed it would be sorted soon. Sea Mother would see to it, just as the ballad foretold.

"Da?"

My father held my hand very tightly as if he also needed convincing. "Things are changing. It's not safe in the city anymore and it's going to get worse. The Fern leader has seized control."

I tugged on his hand and thought how stupid adults were. Craw was forever appointing new leaders, and I didn't believe the Fern one would be any different to the others. "What about Adu? How can she stay in Craw if it's dangerous?"

I could tell he wanted to say something. Probably, my mother had warned him not to spill. Da was a pushover who couldn't deny me anything. Still can't, actually!

He winced and chewed on his lip. "You'll see her soon. Urgh. Very soon."

Two weeks passed in a haze of direness. Ma was a nightmare. She woke early and would return at night, filthy and tired. Grumpy as a spitting cat. All she did was criticise. How I didn't sink into the sand and die a death of misery. The days were very tedious.

"Luce! Sweep the sand out of your room! Can't you wash your own cup? Stop talking back."

On the day everything changed, I'd woken early and read a few pages of the only book in the house—*The Flying Mermaid*. Brought from Craw central by Granma, I believe. It was a fascinating old book. Handwritten in a childish scrawl and illustrated by a great artist. The pictures were bold and strikingly ugly. The mermaids frightful. Just the kind of thing I loved, actually. Each chapter told the story of how a mermaid fought off the forces of evil by using her tail and fishy skills. It included helpful descriptions of the physical act, which I role-played.

Leap and Jump.
Spin.
Flip.

The mermaids had laughable names such as Wonder-Queen, and Tidal-Glitter. How I wished Adu were there to giggle with me.

I was very fired up by the stories of bravery, but they were ridiculously moral, just the same.

Even the smallest person can win the war.

Leap with the waves and find the way of truth.

Nauter-Daughter got there with courage and a pure heart!

Oh, I was wickedly gleeful. "Nauter-Daughter! Ha. Got there, did she? Not stuck in a house filled with spiders. Silly mermaids."

Eventually, I grew bored of being superior, and successfully tiptoed downstairs without waking the adults. It wasn't easy in that decrepit house, which was why I'd mapped a detailed plan of the creakiest boards. When to step left and at what point to hop to the right.

I'm ashamed to say I was an accomplished spy, very used to listening at doors. In those days, everyone whispered. Secrets, secrets, secrets. Da, Granma, and Granda would huddle together down the beach. In the windy garden. Behind the hut. It annoyed me. What were they talking about? How come they knew what I didn't?

When I asked Da, he laughed and hugged me. "Nothing for you to worry about."

I didn't tolerate that kind of nonsense. "Stop squeezing me! I'm not a lemon. You can't make up for ruining my life by talking to me like I'm five years old."

Da's face fell, but he gave me one last squeeze, anyway, to show he didn't bear a grudge. He was good like that, unlike Ma who was as unrelenting as the tides. "It'll blow over. You'll soon be back in school."

Huh. That morning, I'd had enough. Looking back, perhaps I'd been more than a little influenced by *The Flying Mermaid* stories of mutiny and revolution.

I defiantly pulled on my shoes and wrapped a green scarf around my neck—Ma's, nonetheless. Wind rattled the little sea shack we called a house. It was a truly bitter winter.

Though, storms didn't deter me from visiting the beach and watching the seals as I'd done every morning of my life. Adu and I were forever scouring the beaches for treasure and strange objects. One time, we found a big shell that looked like a snail, and inside, crouched a crab. Another, a seaweed bag filled with pearls, Granma said were mermaid tears.

The morning of the mermaids, I legged it out of the house. If Ma or Da had seen, I would've got a shout, I expect. I wasn't supposed to leave the house without telling someone. Not since soldiers had ruined everything. I wasn't supposed to do *anything*.

The dog was waiting at the top of the path. We were already friends and allies and had met on the day we arrived. She'd been hiding in the hut near our house, and cowered when I approached. Poor little thing, she was only a baby. I guessed she'd come with one of the groups of people fleeing the city, and somehow got lost.

I mashed biscuits into warm milk and had been secretly feeding her ever since. I wanted to bring her home, but Ma said no.

"Too much trouble. Too much food. Too much responsibility."

"Too much words," I replied, pulling a face.

When my mother wasn't looking, I stole a blanket from *her* bed, and made the puppy a cosy nest inside the hut.

When she saw me, the dog's tail started wagging so fast I thought she might fly into the air. I picked her up and snuggled her. "Hello, girl!"

Kissed her furry face and soft paws. I loved her, and nothing could have stopped that. Who can ban pure love? Nobody. Not creed factions, or prejudice, or even Sea Mother. Love's as wild as the wind, and every bit as strong.

"I've got your breakfast. Shall we visit the seals?"

She gobbled her food while I stroked her scrubbing-brush fur. I was happy to be free. To be running, and wild, and breathing in good air from the sea. And, yes, to be defying the adults.

When the dog finished eating, we pelted down the steps that weren't really steps but old bits of boats washed up over hundreds of years. Da told me the path had been made by pirates. Once, he showed me jagged flint stuck into the wood and said they were pirate toenails.

The path turned into pebbles, and cold sand, and weed spat out by Sea Mother. I pulled off my shoes and threw them back up the path. I liked the feel of sand under my feet. The patterns and the downward tug.

"We laugh at danger!" I told the dog. "What shall we do today?"

Without my dearest friend, Adu, I confessed all my secrets to the dog. She'd cock her sweet head on one side, and that was how I knew she understood. It wasn't that she'd replaced Adu— nobody could. Just that she was another lonely woman needing a friend.

She scampered ahead. Who suggested the cave? Probably it was the dog. At least, that's what I later told Da. She was an inquisitive little girl who often sniffed out dune tunnels and interesting sea creatures. She was as nosy as me and didn't mind about risk or consequences.

The cave was in the danger zone. Ma had forbidden me to enter, but dog and I didn't care a sea lion's whistle. In low tide, we used to leave presents for mermaids. A flower necklace, a painted fir cone. A pebble moulded by the wind into a star.

We were looking through rock pools and humming, when the dog started barking like she'd never stop. It was the bark of danger. I recognised it because she'd done it that time a soldier chased me on the beach. I never told Ma or Da. He was a shit, and anyway, the dog frightened him away. Horrible soldiers with rules and scary eyes!

I tried to see what had spooked her, but the cave went deep. At that time of day, icy water formed a deep pool.

"What is it?"

I hadn't yet known fear, and still thought the war was a minor inconvenience that could never hurt me, Adu, or my family. Still, I sensed something was nearby. Maybe a ripple of sea foam or a baby seal? Such creatures were often nearby.

"We're not supposed to. It's too dangerous, darling."

I hopped from one rock to another until reaching the cave mouth. Like a true spy, I could never resist the lure of an adventure, and neither could my friend, the dog. I insisted it didn't matter if we got into trouble.

"If Ma finds out! Ha ha."

I held my balance—just—by holding my arms out to the sides and singing. "Hold still, hold still! La, la, la. Hold still, you never will, la, la, la."

I managed to stay upright and jumped the distance from the rock onto the narrow ledge that ran inside the cave. On some days, it disappeared into murky waters. That day, it was still visible.

What happened next became lost in time, war, and denial.

One or two?

Two mermaids, or was one a merman?

How much blood?

The figures were pressed onto the ledge at the back of the cave with heads faced away. In a very short space of time—maybe five seconds—too much happened.

The dog barked.

I lost my nerve.

I wanted my parents.

The body moved its head.

"Help us."

Shocked, I toppled forward and lost my balance. Headlong into the waters I went, with flailing arms and my clothes tangled. I panicked and forgot everything I'd been taught about staying calm. I swam with no heed of the direction of the beach or the huge rocks.

When next my head was above water, I was swept out to sea and fighting for my life. Only then, I remembered Ma's lessons.

"Swim, Wonder-Queen," I shouted and flung my arms out like the mermaid in the book. Although I was used to the ebb and flow, the tide was strong, and things might have gone against me. *I* didn't have a powerful fish tail.

It was the puppy who dragged me inland, with my shirt in her mouth and her paws cleaving through water. When we reached the beach, she wouldn't let me rest or take breath. She saved my life. It wasn't the last time.

I've no recollection of how we got up the path or if we got into trouble. All I remember is sobbing onto my parents and sending them down the path to hunt for the stranded merfolk.

"They need help," I wailed, a cup of something warm between my hands.

My parents were gone for hours, or at least it seemed so to me and the pup. I wrapped her up in a blanket. We cuddled together on the sofa. I brushed her fur, and she licked my chin.

"I'll love you forever. Brave girl," I told her.

Granma and Granda made a fuss of us both, though Granma was rather rude. "What a scruff! She's the ugliest dog I've ever seen. Skinny little thing."

"Shut up! This is my sister. She's as beautiful as a flower. I shall call her Bluebell," I said.

"She's certainly beautiful. Any dog who saves your life is a magnificent one," Granda said, as kind as ever.

Finally, the door opened, and my parents staggered in. They looked different, though I couldn't identify how. Older? Sadder?

"Mermaid news. Well?" I demanded with my usual lack of tact.

"They swam back to sea," Ma said, looking away.

"They were only resting. Don't worry. Who's this princess?" Da said, stroking Bluebell's head. He was a sucker for animals.

To a seasoned sneak like me, the signs were clear. My parents had lied. Ma's hands shook, and for a time, she didn't seem to notice Bluebell on my lap. I wanted to ask, but at the same time, I feared my mother's pale cheeks and wild eyes.

She soon came to her senses and scowled. "Get rid of that dog! We can hardly feed ourselves."

I hugged Bluebell and decided it was time to fight. To the death if I had to! I'd read *The Flying Mermaid* and knew much about battles and loyalty. Women didn't abandon women. Bluebell and I were tied by steely threads. No moany parents would part us.

Fortunately, I didn't have to. Da stepped forward and took Ma's arm. "Arker. This dog saved Luce's life."

Then Granma came to our defence. "All lives are worth saving." She looked keenly at my mother. "Aren't they? Women don't abandon women."

It was a long time before I found out how Granma knew about that line from my book.

She and my mother exchanged a look. Something went between them. Ma smiled, and her expression softened.

"That's a clever dog. The little sweetheart! She'll protect Luce and be company for her," Granda said.

When Ma sighed, I knew we'd won. "All right. But you look after it and keep it out of my way. You know I don't like dogs. And don't let it into your bed! The flea-bitten thing."

Later, Da told me how Ma had been bitten as a child and could never forget her fear. Bluebell seemed to sense this because for a long time she kept her distance from my mother. When the time came for them to be friends, I was the happiest girl alive.

All in all, it had been a long and bewildering day. I'd woken up a lonely child, and went to bed feeling as ancient as the mountains.

"Dead mermaids and almost drowned. We'll be friends forever," I whispered into

Bluebell's furry ears, making sure she was tucked safely into bed with me.

3

Are you still interested, advisor? Or have you grown bored with my account already—vital though it is. Well? I suggest you shake yourself up and keep reading.

A few days after the mermaid incident, I woke to noise. My heart sank. The last time it had happened was when Ma made us leave home and move to the wretched house.

I tossed and turned and considered whether to get up or snuggle back down with Bluebell, who was listening with one eye open.

"What would Tidal-Glitter do?"

Just as I slid from bed to battle the storms, the door opened. Ma, and someone else, hurried in. It was too dark to see. I recognised Ma's scent—a lingering lime she brought back from the sculpture factory—and something else. Oranges! I'd given my dearest friend the perfume on the last festival day before war claimed all fun.

"Adu? Is it really you?"

She leapt into my arms and cried. Because I was spoiled, and ignorant of the facts of the war, I assumed she was upset merely because we'd been parted for such an age—at least four weeks. I stroked her hair, kissed her, and said I'd never let her go again. Then I took off her shoes and coat and popped her into bed with me and Bluebell.

"Adu, this is our other best friend, Bluebell. She's loyal and doesn't like soldiers."

They loved each other from the get-go. Adu stopped crying and *oo'd* and *aa'd*, and Bluebell licked her cheeks. Soon we were cuddled up, with Bluebell in the middle and Adu's head on my shoulder. I thought I might die of happiness. For once, I smiled at Ma instead of cheek and rudeness.

"My life is complete. I don't suppose you brought any books, did you?"

Ma sat on the bed and smiled in a worried sort of way. "There's not much room."

But even my strict mother wasn't mean enough to split us up. After that, Adu and I always slept in the same bed.

My mother made us drink cow breast juice. I forced it down even though it was disgusting.

After Ma closed the door, Adu spilled all that had happened since I left Craw.

"Ma and Da wanted to leave when you did, but we couldn't get out in time. People are fighting on the streets. The scary leader has taken control and wants to kill, kill, kill. The university where Ma works has been razed. They looted the shops and set fire to things. Even soldiers run! Remember Da boarded up the windows? That's how we're alive. I suppose they thought our house was empty, like the others. We waited and waited, and finally, there was a lull. We ran for it."

Her account confused me greatly. Before we left the city centre, things had been strained for ages. Da and Ma worked long hours in the mermaid factory. Even Granma and Granda went. There wasn't much food. All people talked about was war, war, boring war.

Before that, they split the city into three. Ferns took the north, Perthers the south, and everyone else grabbed what they could. Some families, like mine and Adu's, tried to stay strong and remember our lore; insisting divides would deepen the hatred and what we needed was to talk.

"When we left, there was no killing. The divides prevented it," I said slowly.

Adu wept again. "Not any more. It's horrible! Neighbours who've been friends for years are fighting. I didn't think we'd get away. What's going to happen? They say the mayor fled. There's nobody to protect us. All the rules and laws are gone."

I remembered the groups of people that passed our house regularly. Some were ragged and fearful; others frightened me. I hugged Adu, and told her about the caves and the mermaids. I didn't fully believe her desolate account and assumed she'd probably misunderstood. Like always, I thought I knew better. We went to sleep holding hands.

The next day, I showed her the book.

"So bad. Oh dear," she laughed. "Tidal-Glitter!"

"Exactly."

We took it down to the beach and explored rock pools and dunes. Adu was more subdued than she used to be. When a group of people appeared on the horizon, she started trembling.

"We should go back," she said.

"If you want."

When we reached the garden, Bluebell was waiting. When she saw us, she became so excited and giddy that she somehow managed to do a somersault. Adu and I thought it was very good, and cheered and applauded.

"She's like Tidal-Glitter. Flip, girl! Flip!" Adu said.

That's how we decided to train Bluebell to be a mermaid and to follow the commands from *The Flying Mermaid*. Granma and Granda showed us how to reward her with treats and love. By the time Ma and Da got back from work, Bluebell would flip on command and then race around the house barking in a flurry of excitement. Even my mother was impressed.

"Every mermaid is different. Whoever said they couldn't be hairy?" she said, quite correctly.

4

Our time messing about on the beach came to an abrupt end a few weeks after Adu arrived, although it felt much longer. We filled those last days with endless games and indolent pursuits. In the absence of peers and normality, we reverted to using our imaginations. Played in a way we hadn't for years. On the beach, from first light until darkness forced us home. If you'd asked me if I guessed at what was to come, I'd have said no. My faith in Sea Mother was absolute. I knew she'd keep us safe and that our city would soon be healed. Just as the Crawian rhymes told.

Sea Mother, she shall rise.

Adu and I spent our last morning on the beach building a fortress from sea pebbles and damp sand. How well I remember digging out a deep moat, and crafting a bridge from grass. We collected water from the sea, using an old bucket of Ma's, and found stones and shells. Adu crafted human shapes from reeds, and I made mermaids.

"Scaley-Sunrise would insist on having window ledges wrought with thorns. Because she's like that," I said.

Adu agreed and dug out a garden. "And seats crafted from the finest reeds. She'll accept nothing less!"

Perhaps it'll sound strange that ten years later, I think about our fortress often. Like all things created from innocence and youth, it was wonderful. You may say the memory is as vivid now as reality was then. I can smell salty pebbles and picture the vibrant red of the empty crab shell. My heart remembers the deliciousness of being on a Crawian beach, and the slight sting of sand against skin. The sweet purity of having a best friend who loves me unconditionally.

I can't forget, and I don't want to. A fragment of Adu, Bluebell, and I will be on that beach forever; imagining and singing, as young friends do. It wasn't the last occasion we played on the beach, but it was the last time we spent all day alone, and were free. I hope I remember it until my final breath.

Yes. Ten years later, and I'm twenty-three and still miss that fortress. When I told Adu, she kissed me sadly, and said it's not sandy towers I miss, but something else. That the fortress has come to represent home, and the young, hopeful girls we used to be.

Anyway. It was a busy, energetic day. We drank coffee from the flask and ate sandwiches Granda had made. It didn't matter how engrossed they were by events—Granda never forgot to make us lunch before he left for the day with the other adults. Always, he'd cut the bread into sea shapes and give us more than our fair share.

Bluebell snoozed and watched us playing with her head on paws. Since Ma had allowed her to live with us, she'd gained weight and never left my side. All day long, she scurried behind Adu and I joining in our games, wearing mermaid jewellery crafted from pebbles, learning her lessons from *The Flying Mermaid* book.

While we worked, we chatted about the adults. "Where do you think they go all day? Ma won't tell me."

Adu—wrapped inside a towel—fed the last sandwich to Bluebell, who gobbled it up gratefully. "Ma says they're making boats."

She watched me carefully. Perhaps waiting for a chance to share what she knew? Or maybe she was checking my reaction to see if I was upset? It'd been ages since the caves and the mermaids, but I never fully got over it. When I thought of those figures in the water, I wanted to hide. Deep down, I knew the figures hadn't been mermaids, and were likely refugees from the city.

I remember asking myself whether or not I wanted to know about the boats. But I couldn't stand to see Adu so worried.

We never had secrets. I scooted closer and touched the tip of her nose with mine. "Boats? Tell me?"

Although nobody was nearby, Adu whispered rather than spoke. "Mermaid boats and trains. It's a factory."

To be honest, I was disappointed by her answer. I'd been to the factory in Craw hundreds of times. It was a huge, draughty old warehouse. Overflowing with smelly clay, paints, and half-finished statues.

"Why? What's the point, now we're at war? Nobody will buy statues."

"Not statues. *Boats. Carriages. Trains.*"

I was too engrossed in the fortress to listen. Eventually, we grew cold, and went back up the path to our house. We sang songs and held hands, carefree and happy, despite everything.

Bluebell went ahead and disappeared from sight. When she stared barking, I remembered the mermaids and knew something was wrong.

"What is it girl?" I called.

Adu and I rushed up the path and into the garden. By then, Bluebell was barking furiously, and the air crackled with danger.

A uniformed soldier stood in our garden, carrying a bag filled with goods stolen from our kitchen. The glass in the window had been smashed.

When he saw us, he shouted loudly and waved a stick. "Get that dog away! I'm requisitioning this stuff for the troops. You have to do what I say."

When Adu and I talk about it now, she swears I defended us without fear. That's not how I remember it.

I went blank with terror. At the back of my mind was *The Flying Mermaid*, and how, when faced with an emergency, it was imperative to be confident. When Scaley-Sunrise met the pirate ship, she ordered the dolphins to form a defensive battalion.

I intended to do the same. Though my voice trembled, I shouted at the soldier. "Get away from us and put that twig down! Didn't you think of knocking and asking for food? We'd have given you what we have. Don't you know my mother is guardian of the city? She's coming home now, and you'll be in trouble. Get lost!"

I picked Bluebell up, but she scrambled free and stood in front of Adu and me as if she were a big wolf instead of a minuscule puppy. She growled and barked for all she was worth. When the man held up his stick, as if to attack, I was so scared I screamed.

Adu took over. She gripped my hand and shouted, "Fight, Scaley-Sunrise!"

Bluebell shot forward, barking. The soldier dropped everything and tumbled down the sea path.

Adu and I picked up Bluebell and scurried into the house. We locked the doors and the window shutters. We hid under the bed. All afternoon, we expected to hear the door rattle, or gun shots.

When our families got home, we were ordered into the kitchen. Ma retrieved the goods from the garden. The stick had disappeared.

"From now on, you come with us during the day. It's not safe here anymore. Nobody must go down to the beach alone. Trish, when you go to the wind station, take Peta or Aln. The dog can stay and guard the house," she said.

I wasn't exactly happy about the changes, but I was too frightened by what had happened to argue. Bluebell became a legendary heroine, and Adu and I lost another chunk of our childhood.

Much later, Ma told me that the evil leader used kids in a despicable way. Made them shoot guns and do dirty work no adult would do. Took away their choices and consent. I can't be sure, but I think the soldier wasn't that much older than us. A thousand times over, I forgive him for scaring us.

Maybe he was hungry and afraid. I hope he found his way home.

5

Are you still reading, dear advisor? I warn you—the water is about to get choppy. Oh, don't worry. The last thing I want is to upset your comfortable day. Our story doesn't end in tragedy. At least, none that you don't already know.

The next morning, we were woken early and forced to work. My parents and Granma and Granda went in our old car. Adu and I were ordered into the truck. Her parents—Trish and Aln—sat in the front, while we agreed to climb into the open carriage. When Ma wasn't looking, we stowed Bluebell in with us. As if I'd leave her at the spider castle by herself!

The truck was filled with strange items. A huge piece of machinery that rattled with every jolt. Rolls of cloth that felt wet to the touch, and yet were bone dry.

"It's canvas," Adu whispered, gripping my hand.

I was so glad to have her with me, and Bluebell on my lap. The three of us nestled together and tried not to bash into anything.

"What's the cloth for?" I asked.

"Ma won't say. Before the war she used it for boat sails, I think."

"Having a Ma wind researcher is very cool," I said.

The journey to the factory was uncomfortable and fumy. Thankfully, it was over quite soon. I smuggled Bluebell into an old basket we found in the truck and hid her under a blanket.

We clambered out into a grey field in the middle of boring nowhere. Except for a long building that looked like a plane hangar, there was nothing but mountains. Compared to our beautiful beach, it was a wasteland. I was disappointed not to be at the factory in Craw.

I felt sick and rebellious and begged my mother to let us go home. She wouldn't agree, and told us to stay out of trouble and follow her.

"Yes, your highness," I said snootily.

The building was a workshop very like the one in Craw central. In the middle loomed a mermaid structure, as high as a caravan, and as long as a tunnel. I assumed she was yet another statue like the hundreds that lined the streets of Craw.

"Look at her! She's huge," I said.

I recognised people from Craw and spent a while saying hello and asking after my friends. They made much fuss of Adu and me and offered treats and hugs.

"Maybe this wasn't such a bad idea after all," I said, laughing.

Da gave us a quick tour. The building was enormous and on several floors. The rooms were partitioned into different zones, including the sewing machine room and another place filled with broken mermaids.

"Experiments," Da said.

"How long has this factory been here? How come I never came before?" I asked, hurt my parents had been keeping things from me.

Da kissed my cheeks. "A long time. You can help with sealing, and Adu can sew."

Adu went off to the sewing machine room. She was brilliant with stitching, but I didn't have the patience for such delicate work.

Instead, I spent the morning with ten other workers. It seemed the mermaid was almost finished. Da said I had to seal the exterior.

"Don't miss a spot, Luce. It's very important."

I wondered at his serious expression, but I did as he said and became engrossed. Like my mother, I loved art, and could easily switch off my turbulent head while painting or sculpting. Although I had no patience for other delicate tasks, art consumed me.

After a while, there was a commotion underneath a table. The workers laughed and pointed, and others went down to see what was going on.

I knelt to find Bluebell scampering about under our feet. One of the workers found a ball and threw it for her, and I told them she was a mermaid-in-training and a heroine.

"What a darling!" The worker said.

By the time Ma found out, Bluebell was a favourite, and it was too late for her to do anything.

"She's helping. It's very important to keep your spirits up," I said.

The thing I remember most about that mermaid is that she had an expression like thunder. It made me giggle, and I told the workers about *The Flying Mermaid*.

"She looks like Stormy-Spray. Sour and mardy," I said.

I looked around for my ma to see if I was in trouble for bad-mouthing her art, but she was laughing too.

When I finally discovered how important Stormy-Spray was, I remembered that morning and how I'd helped seal the paintwork. It was a delicate job that caused my hands to ache and my back to hurt. But I saw the way the workers paid close attention to the task, and how they respected my mother's work, so I did the same.

At lunch time, I went to find Adu. She was hunched over a sewing machine next to her da. They were humming and their machines whizzed so fast it was dizzying to watch.

"Don't drop a stitch, Adu. Not a stitch," Aln said.

"What are you making?" I asked.

Aln smiled and handed over a package of sandwiches and apples. "A future."

We went outside and ate the lunch and taught Bluebell to sit up. The sun appeared, and sea gulls called and argued. It felt like being back in Craw, where people had always liked to laugh and get together.

I forgot we were miles from home. I never thought to ask where the workers were living now that the city was 'dangerous.' It didn't occur to me that amongst the workers there were people from every creed, or that we were breaking the law by working unsegregated. It was only afterwards I considered such things.

Bluebell was a fast learner and soon learnt her lessons, as well as stealing the hearts of everyone.

"Sit, Stormy-Spray!" I called.

And Bluebell did. When the other workers saw her, they made a fuss and cheered her on. All in all, we had a nice day at the factory. It was tiring and boring sometimes, yes, but the workers told jokes and turned the most tedious of tasks into fun. When I was glum, they told jokes and invented games. I enjoyed the camaraderie and community spirit and realised how much I had missed both.

It haunts me, now. Did those lovely people know what was coming? Were they filled with dread and worry, and if so, how did they manage to hide so much from Adu and me?

Though their names will never be sung about, those people are heroes and heroines. When you drew a list of who to invite into your special circle of niche advisors—did you think to invite them? Did you?

6

Craw advisors—are you still with me? So decent of you to put aside your *important jobs* in order consider my mother's case. I promise to get to the point soon. There's much to say, and none of it easy.

We worked in the factory for most of the week. My fingers grew sore, and so did Adu's. We completed more massive mermaids, each unique. Three had been crafted from some kind of bouncy ingredient. Ma said it was extracted from seaweed, sand, mosses, and new concoctions she'd been experimenting with for ages. I wasn't very interested. I missed the beach and the freedoms Adu and I were used to, and found the days long and tiresome.

Though smaller, Stormy-Spray took more time to complete than the others. The workers said I had to seal her again, and again, and never to stint. When I asked why, a woman called Ambl said it was because Stormy had to be seaworthy. I remembered what Adu had said about boats and worked even harder.

In all my life, I'd never concentrated so well. Perhaps I subconsciously picked up on the urgency that was all around, on the faces of our neighbours and friends, even as they tried to pretend all was fine. In Aln's bleeding fingers after too long spent sewing. In Da's frenzied calculations. Sometimes, when sitting around the long table, paintbrush poised, we'd hear him curse and throw things against the walls in a room nearby.

"Oh, it's nothing! Your da's just a perfectionist. Come and help me with Stormy's lips, Luce. You have such steady fingers," Tigana would say, noting my worried expression.

"Peta! Have another coffee and stop making so much noise!" Another friend, Jin, would yell.

For a while, my father went quiet, and I was able to breathe more easily. Those people did everything to prevent me worrying. Went to so much trouble when their own families were in peril. While Craw balanced on a dangerous brink.

On Friday, Adu's ma—Trish—asked if we wanted to go with her to the wind station instead of the factory.

"Yes! If Bluebell can come with us," I said, though I had no idea where, or what the wind station was.

I ignored Adu, who silently shook her head and crossed her eyes. I always thought I knew best and would ignore advice if I didn't like the sound of it.

"You'll regret it. The wind will make you hurl," she said.

"No. Because I'm as strong as Nauter-Daughter," I said, laughing. That book could always bring us to hysterics. Still does, actually.

We climbed up into the truck while Ma argued about Trish going alone.

"Take Aln. It's not safe outside," Ma said.

Trish, who was as stubborn, refused. "No. It'll be fine. The wind station is on the tip of the cliff. No soldiers ever went, and why would they? There's nothing but machinery and wind."

Ma wasn't convinced. "I'd feel happier if you took Aln. I'd offer to come, but there's too much to do at the factory."

She looked behind her shoulder to check if Adu and I were earwigging. My poor mother hadn't a chance against us. We were experienced spies and had long ago learnt to listen while looking the other way.

"Take the gun," Ma whispered.

My mother hated violence, so it was a shock. I mentally revised the events of *The Flying Mermaid*. There were no guns or weapons of any kind. For some reason, that old book had become our go-to. I constantly compared myself to the mermaids and likened our situation to theirs.

I confided in Adu. "What? Wonder-Queen never used a gun."

She gripped my hand and then kissed my cheek. "That's because she's a mermaid. I don't expect guns work under water. She definitely would have. Wonder-Queen would do whatever she had to."

After that, I felt much better and decided I was okay with Trish bringing a weapon.

Something was agreed between Trish and Ma. They went into the house, and when Trish returned, she brought a big bag Adu and I assumed was filled with rifles and weapons. I even wondered if she'd train us to use them.

We drove for a short while and parked near a long strip of land that jutted out into the sea and went up, up, up. At the very tip, a rectangular building perched precariously.

"It looks like a tongue that's licking the sea," I said, giggling.

"We have to get out and walk now. It's too steep for the truck," Trish said.

As soon as we climbed down, the wind hit us. It was strong enough to take our breath, and we could walk only by bending double. Like strange crabs, we made our way along the tongue of land and into the lighthouse.

Looking forward to being out of the wind, I was disappointed the building had no walls or roof but was a skeleton structure with metallic bars close together. It reminded me of a whale carcass that had been on the beach in Craw.

Trish unlocked the door and ushered us inside. It was the weirdest place I'd ever visited, and filled with whizzing dials and humming machines.

"Don't touch anything," Trish said, noticing me poking at various buttons.

I snatched away my hands and put them in my pockets. "What do they do?"

"Measure the wind."

Trish began taking notes from the dials, while Adu and I petted Bluebell and tried not to get in the way. Strangely, the wind was not so ferocious inside despite no solid walls. I was fascinated and pestered Trish with questions.

"How? How does that work?"

She smiled and showed me around the gadgets. Her scientific explanations were meaningless. It was obvious she hadn't wasted her years at the Mermaid College in Craw.

"This position is unique. Wind arcs merge and create a funnel. Instead of blowing inside, it blasts through the centre, and upwards. That's why there's no roof. It took many attempts to perfect, and even now I'm not certain it's quite right. Would you like to come and see? Make sure you hold on tightly to the banister, and put Bluebell in the basket. I'll carry her. When we reach the top, don't go near the circle."

We climbed a spiral staircase that made me dizzy and nauseous. It wound steeply upwards and appeared to get steeper as it got higher. My breathing grew laborious, and we moved as slow as turtles. I was glad Trish had offered to carry the basket since I became as weak as one time when I had snake disease and was stuck in bed for days.

We finally reached the top. I didn't dare let go of the rails. As Trish said, there was no roof, only a cradle-like structure.

The wind howled and roared, and formed a tunnel that wound up and away into the sky. Until then, I'd never thought about wind as a power that could be harnessed and tamed, but that was exactly what Trish had been researching. Her gadgets and contraptions were cleverly placed to capture the gusts and direct them.

"Watch this." Trish held up a scrap of paper into a circular area surrounded by tubes. The wind devoured it greedily, and it was thrust up into the whirlpool and taken away.

Bluebell became upset and leapt from the basket and into the circle before I could stop her. Immediately, she was snatched by the wind. If Trish hadn't grabbed her, she might've been lost.

"Dive, Windy-Wanda!" Adu shouted.

Bluebell yelped and dived back into the basket. I think that was the easiest of all the lessons she learnt, poor little girl. She's never liked the wind since.

An odd thing happened. Before descending, Trish asked us to stand on a lever and hold the basket with Bluebell inside. She took notes of the gauge.

"What's it for?" I asked.

"I'm weighing you."

Before locking up, Trish left the bag she had brought by the door.

"What about the guns?" I asked.

"Nothing gets past you, does it? Just like your Ma. No guns here, though," she said, winking. Her comment was funny. To me, Ma and I were opposites.

On the drive back, Trish told us she'd been working on the wind station for years and was looking for methods to harness the various slipstreams and gusts of Craw.

"Windy-Wander would be interested. In *The Flying Mermaid* she defeats the evil snakes by asking the gulls to lift her up," I said.

Trish laughed heartily and said she'd heard that story somewhere before.

"Ma wouldn't like it though. She's afraid of heights," I said.

7

7

Are you still awake, dear advisor? I was thinking how 'advisor' isn't such a good title for you to adopt, since you can scarcely advise on a war *you* managed so catastrophically. How awkward!

Might I suggest that ex-leader is a better title?

Anyway. Are you starting to join the dots, ex-leader? I expect you've heard the rumours about what Ma, Da, Trish, and Aln achieved ten years ago. Everyone has. Ma's mermaids are scattered throughout Mainland. Some reached the other side of the world. Her legacy went far, as all acts of kindness and humanity do. This makes me happy, obviously. And sad. It's unthinkable our mermaids won't be united again in our beloved Craw, and Ma won't be able to make new ones since you haven't invited her back.

Sorry. I'm getting ahead of myself. Stay with me. I promise to get to the end soon. It's only that there are things I have to say and people I can't miss out. In war, everyone loses. Even you. I'm sure you understand.

After we visited the wind station, events happened at an alarmingly frantic pace. The days disintegrated into hours and minutes, until our lives were suspended. When I think back now, it seems as if it all happened on one day, but that's not how it was.

Adu, Bluebell, and I worked hard and started going to the factory even at weekends.

Instead of leaving around five, we stayed until dark. A few times, I nodded off across Scaley-Sunrise and woke when Ma shook me to say it was time to go home.

I sensed the urgency that was all around, although I pretended nothing was wrong. It was impossible not to notice sleeping bags and pillows piled in every corner of the factory. The building was filling up with Crawians. People with haunted expressions who kept out of the way and flinched when someone spoke loudly. Kids younger than us, who got excited when Adu and I offered biscuits we'd baked with the last bag of flour.

I averted my eyes from the strain barely below the surface. Doing so was easy—there was more than enough to do, working on Ma's statues. Each was unique and unsettling. Once, I asked Ma why they had to be so ugly, and she told me to forget about ugly and pretty. To think beyond those stifling parameters and accept that worth and beauty are rarely linked. Beauty means different things to each person. I thought deeply about what she said, and came to the conclusion she was right.

The first mermaid to be finished was Squid-Tsunami. She was as massive as a train carriage and every bit as heavy. One time, I bounced a ball against her arms, and it rebounded around the room, with Bluebell hot on its heels. Squid was deceptive and as malleable as rubber, built to sustain and endure. To keep going when everything else has failed. To keep going anyway.

One of the workers told me Ma had shaped her more than a year ago when it became apparent the conflict was likely to get worse. It had taken many months to prepare the statue for what was ahead. My mother guessed what was coming and did her upmost to save as many people as she could.

I didn't worry, or think about, the purpose of the mermaids. That was for the adults to decide, not Adu and me. When we talked in bed, Adu and I guessed Ma was selling the statues to other lands and using the money to help Crawians who were displaced and desperate.

The truth was much cleverer. One day, a worker, Elen, asked me to go with her to the experiment room, where Squid-Tsunami was spread out on a low metallic table. Glad to have a break, I did as she asked.

"Climb up," Elen said.

"Imagine if Squid were to open her eyes and blink! I'd scarper like a rabbit," I said, laughing.

Perhaps you can guess at my surprise when the worker tapped Squid-Tsunami's arm, and a flap popped open above her foot. I leapt back and would've fallen if not for Elen, who had climbed up and caught me as I stumbled.

"Steady," she said.

She led me towards the flap and inside the mermaid, where a labyrinth of rooms was spread out, with lighting and art on the walls. I was astonished at the ingenuity. Fixed seats were positioned with seat belts and blankets. There was even a toilet.

I would dearly have loved to explore at leisure with Adu, but we went to the seats, and Elen asked me to try them for size. I still had no clue what the rooms were for.

"Is it for a museum? How come I never noticed the flap?"

"It's good you didn't notice because that's the way they're supposed to be. We worked on the secret chambers long ago," Elen said, as if her explanation was enough for nosy me.

"But?" I asked.

She sat me on a smaller seat and fiddled with the seat belt. "How does it feel?"

"Comfy. Fun!"

The flap closed, and she asked if I wouldn't mind trialling something. I said I wouldn't mind at all. When we started bouncing up and down, I giggled as if we were at the fair. When the mermaid rocked, I laughed and shrieked, and Elen did the same.

When the motion stopped, Ma come in and asked me some questions. "How long do you think you could sit here?"

I'd always found it difficult to sit still or remain in one place for long. At school, I was often in trouble. My head was filled with too many commands and urges. To teachers, I was a restless nuisance.

"Depends. You know what I'm like! Are there books?" I asked.

Ma laughed. "Yes. Books, toys, food and drink. When you're tired, the seat leans backwards like a bed."

"Still. I don't know if I'd be able to stay in one position for very long. A day? If I had Adu and Bluebell."

Ma screwed her face up in thought. "Okay. So, you'd do it happily and for fun for one day. How about if you had no choice? Could you tolerate it for longer? If you understood that. That—"

She faltered and stopped. I thought her worried expression was part of the game— whatever it was. She didn't wish to upset or worry me.

My mind on *The Flying Mermaid*, I had an answer. "Do you mean if it was life or death? Then I could certainly tolerate it for more than one day. Shiny-Horizon had to tread water in one position for weeks until the sharks swam away. So could I!"

Ma smiled and kissed me and said I'd answered very well. We went back through the flap, and she showed me how the door had been cut into the side of the mermaid.

"Your da designed the chambers. There's an air filter and temperature control system," she said.

8

Still reading? Maybe ex-leader isn't a good name either. Too aggressive. I'm sure you'll agree that we've seen enough aggression for a lifetime. I don't want to create more. How about using the title 'overseer'? I sincerely hope you're seeing inside, as well as skimming the surface.

When the first mermaid left the factory, we cheered as loudly as if she was off to the moon. It was *that* big an occasion. The morning was bright and sunny, with birds singing and the echoes of waves in the breeze.

I wish I could say by then I'd worked out what was going on. Sadly, it wasn't so. It was only during my last minutes in Craw that the pieces of the complex jigsaw slotted together—but I'm getting ahead of myself, dear overseer.

Adu and I had been told to go outside and get some fresh air, and so it was, we missed the preparations. We gladly legged it out the back and spent the afternoon braiding our hair into tentacles and teaching Bluebell to roll onto her back and move her paws as if riding a bike. There was a stream nearby, and some trees, and we had made a swing from some rope. A holiday mood was in the buds on branches and the sweet smell of the heathers. With my besties close, I was happy.

When the great doors at the back of the factory began rolling upwards, Adu and I screamed. Bluebell jumped into the basket and hid herself under the blanket. We'd never seen such a sight before or known the factory was capable of anything like that.

The big reveal was a noisy and slow process. Workers stepped from the factory and out into sunshine. Some with children and older relatives, others with arms linked. I noticed that some brushed tears from their eyes, but I explained it away with over-bright sunshine.

A truck appeared, towing a long carriage like a train. After a complicated set of manoeuvres, Salty-Starfish was lifted onto the carriage and securely attached. Another truck brought up the rear. Engraved on the sides of the vehicles and the carriage was my mother's mermaid symbol as guardian of the city.

Ma jingled a set of keys. "I'll sit up front, in case of trouble. Peta will drive behind in the car."

Eln stepped in immediately. "No, Arker. It's gotten too risky. Frian will drive. You need to stay here with your family. Nobody should split up now. It's too late for that."

My mother wouldn't agree. "As guardian, I'm guaranteed passage, and they can't argue with that. They'll let us through—the fools think the money for the statues is coming to them. Once past the guards, I'll slip out and find Peta. Then we'll drive back."

Except for the sky, beach, and sea, our city is surrounded by steep mountains that cannot be crossed. The sea was guarded by guard ships. There's only one way in and out of Craw and that's through the Gatehouse. Either by road, bridge, or by train, the passenger had to exit or enter via our ancient monument.

We fussed, getting Star-Fish ready. I washed her face, and Adu pulled hard on the ties that secured her.

Finally, Ma got into the truck, and they set off with Da behind in the car. They didn't leave quietly. We rushed forwards and cheered and clapped.

"Go with speed, Salty-Starfish!" I shouted.

The workers heard, and repeated the call. When the mermaid left the building, our shouts were so loud I'm quite sure Sea Mother would've heard.

As soon as the entourage vanished from sight, Trish and Aln rushed Adu, Bluebell, and me inside their truck.

"Where are we going?" I asked.

Nobody answered. We sped back towards the house, though it was early yet, and not time to pack up work for the day.

I was relieved to have a rest and decided not to argue. I snuggled up with Adu, and we agreed to persuade Da into going down the beach when we got home to check on our fortress.

"Maybe we can go home soon? I mean our real home," I whispered.

"I hope so!" Adu replied.

To our surprise, we didn't go straight to the house. Instead, Trish drove us to the wind station. She ushered us inside despite our protests, though she let Bluebell stay in the truck in her basket.

"I don't want to go. It made me so dizzy," I complained.

"It's important. Just five minutes. Hurry," Trish urged.

It was rare she was so stern or severe. Trish was a jolly woman who'd known me all my life and was good at making me laugh.

We struggled up the spiral staircase, with the wind attacking us on every side. Just like last time, I was weighed down and forced to walk like a turtle with a great weight on my back. It took ages to reach the top.

We clung to the rails, and Aln handed out long tubes. He showed us how to look through the glass and explained how they were devices that enabled you to see a long distance. "Out there. Do you see the Gatehouse?"

I squinted and sighed and blinked. My binoculars were out of focus. I fiddled until suddenly, the visage cleared, and I seemed to be looking directly at the Gatehouse entrance point.

"It looks like it's right here!" I exclaimed.

"Watch. The trucks will arrive soon," Trish said.

I swivelled, looking at this and that. It had been ages since we left Craw, so it was exciting to see the beach and the bridge where Granda and Granma used to take me on Sundays.

Aln shouted first. "There it is!"

Although I didn't fully understand the implications of the situation, I picked up on Trish and Aln's fear and anticipation. Aln was beside himself and jumping up and down. Trish breathed heavily and clutched at Adu.

It was then I noticed what happened between every vehicle that crossed the bridge. Whether it was a train, boat, walker or car, a great gate came down and slammed shut the path. Guards wearing various uniforms swarmed the vehicle, and it was a few minutes until the gate went up and the person got through.

"Why?" I asked.

"They're only letting certain people leave the city," Trish said. "Six months ago, the gate was open to all. Leaving Craw was easy. Ansars were the first creed to be stopped. Next it was Skarles. Last month, it was Perthers. This week? Today? Who knows."

She finished the sentence by shrugging her shoulders.

I didn't understand and couldn't see what the problem was. I had never wanted to leave Craw in the first place. "But why?"

We watched as the car in front of the truck and Salty-Starfish approached. The gate came down, and the car was surrounded by soldiers holding rifles.

What happened next has become blurred over time. People were dragged from the car. Gunshots exploded. Soldiers drove the vehicle back into Craw.

As the truck towing the mermaid inched forwards, I remembered my mother was in the front seat. It could only have been seconds, and yet the process seemed to take forever. I heard Trish's voice saying, quite clearly that Ma was getting out and holding up her forever pass—awarded by the mayor when I was a baby.

Always clumsy, I dropped the binoculars. Adu started shouting and cheering. "Go on Salty-Starfish! You can do it!"

Trish and Aln shouted, too, so I joined in. By the time I held the binoculars against my eyes, the trucks had crossed the gate, and Salty-Starfish was on her way to a safer place. My mother had disappeared and was presumably walking back into Craw to meet Da.

On the drive back to the house, Trish said a strange thing. "Now you know. It's life and death, as you said. There'll come a time when you have to sit still."

9

After that, our moods deteriorated, and the world was less bright. The factory seemed vast and empty without the sleeping bags and the many children who'd disappeared with Salty-Starfish. Adu and I crept into the workstations, as flat and depressed as the other workers who hung their heads, diminished by the departure.

Despite everything, my loyal Crawian friends had energy and heart enough to tell jokes for our benefit and sing the songs we liked best. Granma and Granda brewed endless rounds of hot drinks that nobody wanted. At lunch time, Da offered to play hide-and-seek. Elen allowed us to choose the colours for the mermaids. Adu and I got more attention than ever, and yet a mist obscured the skies and our future.

When I asked after the whereabouts of the missing people, the only answer I received was an offer of yet another drink.

I know what you're asking, dear overseer. Is it possible I didn't know what was going on? The answer is complicated, as are all such matters of the heart. It wasn't that I hadn't seen violence erupting on every corner of Craw. Like everyone else, our street had been labelled and sectioned off. Remember—I'd already lost my real home, most of my friends, and gotten used to working instead of attending school.

It wasn't that I'd lived in a protective bubble. Neither was I stupid. But I had absolute faith in Sea Mother, and simply couldn't imagine she'd let people tear our city apart.

"It'll be all right. Won't it?" I asked Adu.

She brushed Bluebell's hair and tied a blue ribbon above her ears. "I don't know. Who's even in charge? Remember when there was a mayor? She fled the city and stole our supplies of money. She left the tyrant in charge. All he wants to do is have power and control over the mines."

It was confusing. We reached for the comfort of *The Flying Mermaid*. At lunchtime, Adu found a chapter where the mermaids got into a fight about territory. They were ordered to the palace of the Queen of the undersea, Brilliantine-Seahorse.

We told ourselves it was Bluebell's idea to roleplay. Adu and I checked none of the workers were listening. Although we were allowed to play, we wanted to be thought of as adults instead of young girls.

I took the part of the queen, and Adu the mermaids. I blew my chest out and wore a crown of wild flowers. "What do you have to say for yourselves, Scurvy-Flotsam?"

Adu burst into laughter and struggled to hold it together. "Oh, Majesty! I'm sorry we fought, but it's not my fault."

"How so?" I demanded.

"Because Sticky-Crabface stole my job as a hair stylist."

I was bent double from laughter and so was Bluebell. "Sticky-Crabface! Ha ha ha."

We played outside for much longer than we should. Our roleplay led to the formation of a system of punishment and consequence we called the 'speak-and-listen.' I suppose we got the idea from school, where teachers had always said if both sides told the truth and listened, then our classrooms would be a better place.

The skies darkened, and we turned away from the stage we'd created from old crates. I was shocked to find Ma listening with an expression difficult to decipher.

"We were just coming!" I said, assuming we were in trouble.

But it wasn't the case. My mother hugged Adu and me and ushered us inside.

"Speak-and-listen. Wouldn't that be good?" she said.

The next mermaid to leave was Sparkling-Sponge. Another one destined for the road, she was massive and well-padded, outside and in. Adu and I tested the seat belts and were allowed to choose some books from the piles that lay at the far end of the work station.

I picked adventure stories with bright illustrations. "These. I'd look at the pictures for hours."

I sadly worked out what the books were for and why Adu and I weren't allowed to take them home. We solemnly left them inside Sparkling, taking care to wipe the covers clear of dust.

The departure happened the same way as the last time. Elen tried to talk Ma into staying behind, and my mother refused. When Sparkling left the factory, we cheered and shouted and whistled her on her way.

That time, I ran to Trish's truck without being asked and was careful to bring Bluebell's basket. I willingly climbed the spiral stairs and watched as Ma successfully got through the Gatehouse which was crowded with soldiers.

Behind, long trails of smoke blew into the sky. The city was on fire.

"It's burning. The time for negotiations is gone. Will we be in time?" Aln said, sighing.

"We can do it. The other factories are complete and empty. There's hardly anyone left," Trish murmured, glancing aside at Adu and I.

We, of course, looked steadfastly ahead as if not interested in what she had to say. Later, in bed with Bluebell, we clutched one another and tried to hold on to all that was left.

10

Almost done, dear overseer. Might I suggest an alternative title? Now you know about the speak-and-listen, mightn't you consider adopting the term, 'listener?' I know you'll agree that our damaged city cannot possibly be healed until the people who took part in the wars are heard. Until the conversation about all that happened has been initiated.

After writing this letter, I feel we know each other well. Although I despise your bogus position of power, I wish to protect you from what's to come. What can I say? I'm Crawian through and through. I learnt our ways when I was a baby, as did you.

The way of Craw is the way of the sea.
Sea Mother protects her children.
Storms kill.

The way of the sea isn't cruel, and neither am I. That doesn't mean there isn't pain and suffering beneath the waves. The sea is relentless, and beautiful, and terrifying because it must be and has no other way.

Still, I hope this letter doesn't cause you too much discomfort. Sit down, please. Take a few breaths before we go on together. Think. Reflect. Listen to the Crawian birds and know that I imagine them every night as I fall asleep and again as I open my eyes.

If I close my eyes and concentrate, I can hear the Crawian beach birds as if they're right here. The low, long call and the high mocking laughter. The toot-toot and the peck-peck-peck. Throughout my childhood they were as constant as storms and sun. I've not heard those calls since. I miss them. In Farland, where we live now, the birds sing different songs. Pretty, yes. Familiar? Family? No, and no.

Anyway. We had an evening of last times. Adu and I didn't know it was the end of our time in Craw, or if we did, we didn't talk of it. Da took us down the path with pirate toenails. Our fortress was in pretty good shape, so we spent a while reinforcing her walls and bridges even further. I wished I was small enough to live within those walls that were made from play and love.

We walked into the sea, up to our knees and talked to Sea Mother about the smoke and the soldiers. The gunshots and refugees who still walked past the house, with nowhere but mountains to go. The fear opening up inside me like a ragged ravine.

"Keep us safe, dearest Sea Mother," Adu said.

"And the ones who left inside the mermaids. Please help them find new homes with no war. Sea Mother won't let them down. Will she, Da?"

My father put an arm around us and gazed into the horizon. "No. But maybe she won't help in the way that you'd like. Sea creatures are wild and free, and she's no different."

Adu and I took offense at his serious tone and splashed him. It quickly turned into a water fight, with Bluebell darting in and out of the waves.

When we staggered back up the path, we were soaking wet, ruddy with cold, and easier in spirit. The tension had been released by our screams and shouts.

I wish I could recall the last night in bed. Whether Adu and I brushed each other's hair, or if we read our palms for fortunes. She swears we didn't do either—that we were far too tired and simply snuggled into sleep with Bluebell.

11

The next day, we finished the last mermaid. Perhaps it should have been a sombre occasion, but it was anything but. We were giddy and reckless. Elen 'accidentally' painted Gleaming lips of different colours. Granma added some silver streaks to her hair, and *still* the mermaid was a scary monster.

"I think she's the ugliest of them all. Sorry, Gleaming-Oyster, but it's true. You're a fright. We love you anyway," I said ruefully, kissing her arm.

Heaving Gleaming onto the carriage took a long time—there were fewer workers, and she was heavy. Even with the specialist machinery Da had designed, we struggled. I remember wondering if it was an omen, and that instead of escape, we should fight to reclaim our city.

Gleaming was finally secured to the carriage. We helped the last people climb inside and clipped tight their seat belts. Goodbyes were painful. There were no games or jokes.

"Be safe. Write to us. One joyful day, the war will be over, and we'll be together again on the city beach. We'll sing the ballads on the eve of the new year, and all will be well. One day. Don't forget us," I said, lingering at the flap before it was sealed.

I shouted myself hoarse as Gleaming and the trucks drove away, leaving clouds of dust.

After that, only Elen and my grandparents remained. I had forgotten about the smaller mermaid, Stormy-Spray, that had required so many coats of varnish.

"What about you, Elen? Are you coming back to Craw with us?" I asked.

She shook her head. "I've got one last, very important job. What do you mean you're going back to Craw?"

Adu and I had regularly discussed the time after the mermaids. She said my mother would drive into Craw and demand to see the tyrannical leader, who had apparently taken control of the city and the precious mines for which Craw was famous. I argued that Ma was a doer, not a talker. I was sure the time had come for Sea Mother to rise—like in the ballad. Maybe she'd drown the evil leader?

Sea Mother, she shall rise.

We didn't follow Gleaming's departure through the Gatehouse. Trish, Elen, Aln, Granda, and Granma busied themselves out back, while Adu and I began tidying the factory. We piled what was left and talked about what was for dinner.

It was only an hour or so later that we heard Da's car screaming up the drive and the rude honking of the horn.

12

Buckle up, dear listener. The storm's here...

We ran outside as the car skidded to a halt. Ma stuck her head out of the window. Her hair was awry from the scarf she normally tied around her head. There was something wrong with her face.

She yelled the words. "They're following us! Now! It has to be now."

There was a scramble for seats. Adu and I grabbed Bluebell's basket and dived into the car. Elen, Trish, Aln, and my grandparents made for the truck. Granda struggled to keep up and fell to the dirty ground. I offered to help, but Da slammed my door shut.

"Stay in the bloody car," he shouted, with a voice breathless and tight.

I was scared and shocked. Da had never shouted at me before, or since. I was sure when Sea Mother heard, she'd let lose a storm so bad it would wash us all away.

Elen helped him into the truck. Poor Granda! Even before the war, he was frail. Both grandparents had worked in the mines when young and been left with weakened lungs.

For years, it worried me that he'd wonder why I didn't help him. Now, of course, I know he'd never have thought such a thing.

The vehicles set off at speed. Adu and I clutched at one another, and Bluebell hid inside her basket. When the car turned left—away from the city—I leaned forward into the space between my parents.

"Aren't we going into Craw to wait for Sea Mother?"

I turned to look out of the back window. Aln drove the truck with my grandparents up front. I waved. Nobody waved back.

We headed in the direction of the wind station. I wanted to ask where we were going. I was confused and upset and, for once, silent. Adu hugged me and wiped away my tears, and Bluebell darted out to lick my hands.

Da turned off the road onto a rough track I'd never seen before. It was directly before the jutting tongue and the wind station, which loomed far above.

The car came to a skidding halt on a pebbled track that wound down to the sea. The truck followed. The tide was high, and there were mere inches between the water and us.

"Stay in the car, girls," Ma said.

The next few minutes were frenzied. Elen, Aln, and Trish threw back the canvas on the truck to reveal Stormy-Spray. It was obvious they'd practised the manoeuvre, for within minutes they'd wheeled her off, and onto the beach.

Elen dragged a small powerboat from beneath the overhanging reeds and attached it to Stormy. Within minutes, she was in the boat with the engine running. My grandparents started hugging everyone. A lead sensation pulled on my stomach.

"They're going to tow Stormy to sea," Adu whispered.

"But. There's only room for one person. Two at most. We can't all fit," I said.

I forgot about being shouted at and went out onto the beach. Granma and Granda surrounded me in kisses and cuddles. They told me they loved me and that we'd soon be together again. Granda told me not to be good and never to be quiet. I wrapped myself around him and wouldn't let go. When Da lifted me away, I'm ashamed to say I kicked out.

Everyone had a unique, personal, moment of when the war started. Before and after became separated and will always be used as a point of reference.

Before then, we walked freely on the streets. After that, we ate every two days.

For some, it was when school closed. For others, when the barricades came up, or after the first gun shots were fired.

For me, it was when my Granda and Granma clambered into Stormy without us. It was then I understood what war brings, and very how much it takes.

"Why can't they come with us?" I cried.

"Granda's breathing is too poor. He's not strong enough," Da said. "It's better for him this way."

Elen steered the little boat, and Ma and Da pushed Stormy across the pebbles and into the low water. She soon bobbed free of their hands. It was a rough day with angry waves and screaming wind. When Stormy was tossed and turned, I sobbed anew.

Ma tried to comfort me. "Stormy is well padded. They won't feel a thing! Their ride will be short and comfortable. Elen is aiming for Farland, where Aunty Merle will be waiting on the beach. They'll be okay. They'll be with Aunty for breakfast. Elen is the best boat mistress of Craw. She can steer through waves as good as any dolphin."

"What about sea soldiers? It's forbidden to take boats into the open waters," Adu said.

"They're busy in the city. Nobody is paying attention," Da replied. He pointed to the west, where smoke was billowing into the skies.

"They'll be okay. They'll be okay. They will," Ma said, enough times that I understood she was as terrified as me.

They got quite a way out before the boat stalled. Elen knelt over the engine. Stormy sank, with bubbles and gurgles, and so did we. Onto the wet pebbles on our hands and knees.

Ma was inconsolable. She flopped into a heap and wept. My strong mother: who defied soldiers daily to get others to safety, who ruined her hands making statues of hope for the children.

"My own parents! What have I done?" she cried.

I thought about the many times I sealed the mermaid. How the strain hurt my back and fingers. How we never stinted or missed a spot.

It was me who stood and walked into the shallow waters. With all my might, I shouted and punched at the air.

"Stormy-Spray! Get out here and do your job. Do you hear me? This is no time to be having a rest. Get up immediately."

One by one, the others copied.

Finally, Ma joined us and gripped my hand tightly. "Get your stupid face out here, Stormy-Spray! You lazy hag! Move it!"

Adu and I laughed and cried. We'd never heard Ma say a bad word about a mermaid before.

Dear listener, have you seen a dolphin explode from the water? The way the water breaks and froths like a volcano waiting to burst free? The joy that's in the arch of the body and the flip of the tail. Onlookers can't help but be happy and hopeful. You've seen wonder and freedom and will be forever changed.

That's what happened. Elen got the engine working. There was a sudden and explosive burst of white and blue. Stormy erupted from the waters. She dived upwards and arced back down to bob safely on the waters. Elen waved one last time and then sped away.

Trish and Aln headed back in the direction of the vehicles. The rest of us cheered and shouted until Stormy disappeared from sight. Da led us over to the cliff and pointed towards a steep and rickety path that led up to the wind station.

"Climb," he said. "Faster than you've ever moved."

13

It was a terribly hard climb. Bluebell ran on ahead. By the time we reached the top of the cliff, we were gasping and faint from exertion. Although we'd come far, the wind station was still above us. From within, we could see the figures of Trish and Aln.

"What are we doing here?" I asked. "Shouldn't we stand with Sea Mother and fight?"

Da ushered us to the base of the tower and the door. We staggered around the corner and took a minute to catch our breaths. Wind beat our heads and ears. I was dizzy from the climb and the emotion of the day. Adu threw up.

A car appeared over the brow of the hill and came to a halt. It was filled with young soldiers. Before we could move, one got out waving a rifle. Another followed and stood behind the first.

To this day, I remember the coldness of the boy's expression. The hatred. The meanness and spite. The lack of humanity. The greed.

And fear. Behind him, a carful of soldiers laughed when he stuttered. Now, I understand the pressure he was under from those fools. Perhaps his own life was in jeopardy. I don't believe war makes people cruel when they were not so before, but I know it can make them weak. Wicked people use those who are vulnerable, or conflicted.

"Arker Fi. You're under arrest for hiding prisoners and are an enemy of the state of Craw. You're to come with us to be tried," he said.

"How old are you? Don't you know me, darling? Haven't you got a mermaid figurine?" Ma said.

The boy faltered and rubbed his eyes. The soldier hiding behind stood to one side and raised her hand. Something flew through the air and spliced a nearby tree trunk. It was a knife.

"Mermaids, rubbish. We can't eat mermaids," she said.

My mother seemed to shrink. I clung to her hand and silently begged Sea Mother to help us. Da tried to reason with the soldiers. For a while, I believed all would be well and my da would be able to sort it out, like always. When the boy aimed the rifle towards my mother, I understood it wasn't the case.

"Get in the car. Move!" he barked, emboldened by cheering from the direction of the car.

Bluebell rushed out from wherever she'd been, as fast as a lightning streak. She hated soldiers and could never resist barking at anyone in uniform.

"Fight!" Adu shouted.

Bluebell dashed in and nipped the boy on the ankle. He ran back to the car. The girl had disappeared.

"Run!" Da shouted.

We tore around the tower towards the door. When I looked for my dog, she was gone.

"Bluebell?" I shouted.

"She'll come," Da said, pushing us inside the tower. "Up!"

I had no reason to disbelieve Da, so I ran as fast as my tired legs would go. Up, up, up into the tower, with my chest burning and vision blurred.

Our shoes clanged and crashed on the metallic steps. From above, Trish and Aln shouted that we should run faster.

We crowded onto the roof and saw what had not been visible from the ground—an air balloon and basket, suspended by the wind. Now I understood what the cradle with the ladder was for.

Trish tugged at levers and dials, and Aln was hanging off one of the chords that prevented the balloon from flying off into the skies.

"Get in. Up! Inside the heart of the mermaid," Trish shouted.

We clambered up the ladder and into the basket, which was bigger than it looked. It was violently swayed and rocked by the wind.

"Bluebell!" I shouted.

I tried to get out of the basket, but Ma wrapped herself around me like a giant squid.

"She'll be all right. She'll be all right," she kept saying.

"First ties," Trish yelled.

Aln and Da released some of the bindings while I wriggled to get free. The basket lurched upwards, and the wind howled. Trish hopped from one side of the basket to the other, leaning, and moving levers and gadgets.

"I can't leave without Bluebell. Please?" I said, sobbing into my mother's hair.

We heard the clattering of steps and guessed the soldier was climbing the spiral stairs.

"Second ties. Hold on," Trish yelled.

Aln released more ties and the basket shot upwards, and was suspended in the air by the gusts. Only two bindings prevented us from being propelled into the sky.

14

Dear listener, it's ten years since, and still, I wake with the echoes of Bluebell's barks ringing in my ears. How she got past the soldier on the stairs, I don't know. Did the soldier see her running under his feet and decide to let her go?

Or perhaps she flew past without him noticing, for she was fast when desperate. Whenever we were apart, she'd look for me and grow frantic with worry. My dear little dog knew what it was to be left behind and wasn't about to allow it to happen again.

"Bluebell!" I shouted.

"Final ties!" Trish yelled.

Aln cut one tie, and the basket lurched and pulled to be free. Trish, who was standing, suddenly pointed towards the stairs. "Bluebell! There she is. Come on, girl. We can reach her!"

I fought to stand upright and then looked over the edge of the basket. Bluebell was up on hind legs at the top of the spiral stairs. Barking desperately. I tried to reach her, but the distance was too great.

The basket shook and swung dangerously, caught now by only one binding. Trish moved the levers and hopped from side to side.

"I can bring us down a bit. Arker, you'll have to be quick," she called to Ma.

Ma and Trish have been friends since little girls, just like Adu and I. They share a secret language and can say much with one word or gesture. Even with wind louder than thunder and consuming panic, they understood one another.

With difficulty, Ma stood. She'd always hated heights. My father must've guessed what she had planned and tried to convince her otherwise.

"It's too dangerous, and we need to go. Bluebell will be okay. She's clever and sweet. She'll find new owners. We have to go while the wind is strong. Go, Trish. Don't delay!"

The boy's head appeared at the top of the stairs. At the same time, Trish brought the basket down a little.

"Now!" she shouted.

Ma looked between me and Da. "We don't leave a woman behind. Catch my feet."

And she threw herself over the side of the basket. Only the most powerful love would make someone act so—between that of a mother and her child.

Da and Aln grabbed her feet. My mother stretched, and leaned, and shouted down at Bluebell.

"Mermaid, flyyyyyyy!"

My good girl! Without hesitation Bluebell leapt into the wind. The poor baby spun and was tossed as if in a whirlpool. The distance was too far. It seemed she would fall back and be plunged to her death. In desperation, she moved her paws as if swimming to me.

The boy aimed his gun towards the sea and fired, far from us.

Right then, the girl who had thrown the knife appeared at the stair top, pushed past the boy, and tripped. She scrambled to her feet and stared upwards at us.

I caught her eyes, and she caught mine. She wasn't a vicious killer, but a girl just like me.

She looked between me Bluebell. Somehow, she understood how much creatures meant to me. Because she was the same. Her connection to animals was stronger and more profound than war, or anything foul that had been done to her.

I mouthed *please*.

It was over in a second. She reached up on tip-toes and caught Bluebell.

"Anees!" the boy shouted.

The girl made a ragged run-up and then threw Bluebell forcefully into the wind stream. For a second or two, my darling pooch really did fly. Ma managed to clutch her by the scruff of the neck. Trish released the last binding and adjusted the lever.

At the last moment, I shouted down. "Thank you!"

We shot up into the sky faster than a shooting star. I honestly don't know how we pulled Ma and Bluebell into the basket, but we did. Crisis and hysteria will lend anyone strength, and we had eons of both.

Everyone sobbed. Bluebell fled underneath my jumper and didn't come out for many hours. Ma collapsed onto the floor of the basket, laughing.

"Never. We never leave a woman behind," she said.

But, we already had.

15

War! Was it worth it? So much was lost and left behind. Precious lives. Houses and friends, safeties and freedoms. Childhoods and dreams. All that, yes. And yet, as our balloon blasted off into the cloudy skies, I only thought of the chestnut-haired girl we'd left in the wind station.

"She's our friend forever. Forever, I tell you! I wish we could've saved her," I said, cuddling Bluebell and crying into her hair.

"Me too. We'll find her, I promise. One day we'll meet her again and take her into the sea. I promise. We'll make her a mermaid," Ma said.

We reached for one another. A girl and her ma. Love so powerful and profound. Ten years later and I'll never forget, or leave, that moment of togetherness. It holds me, always.

Da got out his maps then and discussed the route with Trish. "The wind is strong. Everything's in our favour. We'll follow the ocean down south and rest in Breen. With luck and Sea Mother's will, we'll land with the mermaids in Berker Park. Nila should have arrived by now."

Together, they leaned and pushed and tamed the balloon. For a few hours, they wrestled and were unable to control the direction of our journey. It was the first time Trish had steered a balloon, after all.

For ages, we floated inland and bobbed dangerously close to the mountains. Clever Trish eventually managed to turn us around and back to the coast.

It didn't take long for our energy to return. Adu and I, with Bluebell snuggled inside my jumper, gazed out at the world that looked like a child's toy. When we reached Craw, we were dismayed at the thick, heavy smoke that hung across the city. As if a dragon had seared the city and then abandoned it. Fire was everywhere.

Here it is, dear listener. Deep breaths. We've arrived at the terrible occurrence that obliterated Craw. Some say it was Sea Mother's wrath, but you know better. It was caused by people like you. The international army made the decision to activate the device trigger, yes, and many others contributed to that decision. The cruel Fern leader. The mayor, who abandoned her people and looted their wealth. Every Crawian who shunned the Ansar refugees and plotted to keep them out. Ferns—Perthers—each creed that wanted dominion, and control of the mines. Everyone who gave way to selfishness and forgot that all peoples and creatures are connected.

Things were going well up to then. We'd just blown across the city towers when *it happened*. A vapid darkness that consumed the city and the ocean. The deafening noise and howling wind. Poison that spilled far into the ocean, and lightning streaks that ripped the skies apart.

As one, we covered our ears and tried to shield ourselves from the bolts of light that Sea Mother hurled. Bluebell trembled, and whined, and wrapped herself around my neck.

"What is it?" Adu and I cried.

I honestly thought Sea Mother had cracked open the world, and everyone and everything would die. In some respects, my guess wasn't far wrong.

"Oh, my heart. A poison bomb," Da said, quietly, and with force.

The blackness spread throughout the city, down the coast, and into the sea. For many miles, that obscene and wicked stain of horror gobbled up all the colour and goodness that constitute our good earth.

It didn't look as if we could possibly survive. Against such powerful electrical lightning, our balloon shrank, and shrivelled, and struggled. We lost height and drifted down towards the water.

Trish flung herself from one side of the basket to the other, pulling at levers and gadgets. Anything to keep us afloat. Years later, she admitted she reacted from instinct rather than knowledge, and that she didn't believe she could save us.

Aln sat between Adu and me with an arm around our shoulders. Both stared up into the canvas as it heaved and contracted.

"Hold. Hold! Not a stitch, Adu, my darling, my baby. We didn't drop a stitch," Aln whispered.

"Not a stitch, Da. We didn't drop a single stitch," Adu replied, with tears running down her cheeks.

Ma forgot about her phobia of heights and squared up to the horror. When she shouted, it was with fists clenched and a fearlessness I'll remember always.

"Fools! What have you done? The sea is poisoned and ruined. The dolphins and seals? The whales? Sea Mother will never forgive us or let us back. Don't you know her curse? Craw will wither!"

Somehow, we got through it. Trish ignited a light, and the balloon shone brightly through the gloom. The mermaid that Adu and I had painted so carefully drifted past the city and down the coast. The last light, before the longest and most bitter of nights.

My mother screamed her goodbyes into the smoke and poison of Craw. "I'll come back for you, children! Don't forget! Don't give up! One day, one day. I'll come back for you! Remember me."

16

It's impossible to go inside a mermaid's heart and be unchanged, or unmoved. Our journey ripped us from home and roots, from family and identity. It was hard, and cold.

We were lucky, and stayed afloat. Our trusty balloon moved one inch at a time through the sludge the bomb left behind. After many hours, the air became fresh, and the ocean returned to its natural colours.

Ma hugged Adu and me close. We fell asleep. Someone covered us in blankets. When I awoke to snow, I saw the bag Trish had brought, and it was filled with food and supplies. She saw me looking, and smiled.

"No guns," she said.

After a while, Bluebell peeped out and accepted some food. She cheered up and seemed to forget about what had happened. It didn't take long before she moved freely about the basket, sniffing and playing. It was then that she and Ma become friends.

It was freezing. We had to stamp our feet to stay warm. Trish's muscles cramped from leaning into the wind, and everyone was thoroughly exhausted.

I found out what had happened at the gate. Ma told us how Gleaming-Oyster had passed through the gate and at the last moment, her door popped open. She made it through, but soldiers chased Ma all the way to the factory.

It was years before we knew the truth about the bomb. A soldier exploded the road and train lines. Fearing the same fate would befall the precious fuel mines, the International Army detonated the poison bomb. It was more destructive and far-reaching than they had anticipated. It leaked into the ocean and rivers, and found Sea Mother. The rest is history.

During our journey, we talked of the past. My mother was found on Craw beach when only a day or two old, and adopted by Granma and Granda. A true mermaid sent into Craw by Sea Mother. She and Trish had written *The Flying Mermaid* when they were girls, with nothing much to do, and too much to do.

For days, we followed the coast in a southerly direction. Da scrutinised his maps, and Trish worked tirelessly to keep us afloat.

The weather started to change. One day, the sun appeared, and Da pointed excitedly at a crescent-shaped beach. It was time to head inland.

We landed in Breen quite soon after. Trish and Da used up the last of their energy directing the balloon and bringing us down from the clouds.

We saw twenty statues from above. I couldn't help shouting and waving, for those tall women were family to us. I saw Gleaming-Oyster, standing up, straight and proud as a mountain.

Clever Trish brought us down inch by inch until the basket landed. When we were finally safe, she curled up and fell asleep at last.

Nila and our friends from the factory were waiting. They told us that, as far as they knew, every mermaid had survived and so had the people inside. Some had already walked into Breen to seek work and accommodation—others had moved on to other towns and cities.

We stayed for one night and slept inside Gleaming-Oyster. I found a scented scarf that belonged to Granma and found much comfort in it. For years, I slept with that scarf hidden beneath my pillow.

When Da said we had to set off again the next morning, I cried and refused to get inside the basket. I couldn't bear to leave Gleaming behind. With her strange lips and silver streaks that Granma had painted, she was the last connection we had with Craw.

"Why can't we stay here?" I asked.

"Because there's another place with boats, where we can sail to Granma and Granda. A safe place."

Still, I didn't like it. I sat on the grass with arms crossed and refused to budge. To everyone's surprise, it was Bluebell who changed my mind. She scurried over to the basket and hopped in through the open gate. After that, I went willingly.

Trish and Da ignited the wind engine that Adu and I had once found in the truck. It stalled several times, and for a while, it seemed as if we would be staying in Breen, after all.

The engine finally spluttered into action and forced gusty winds inside the balloon. The basket was dragged along the grass, us screaming inside, before being lifted up into the sky. The last I saw of Breen was Gleaming-Oyster's silver streaks.

Our balloon landed a day later in Crinera. We lived. We went on. Endured. Adu and I attended school. We had to learn a new language, and it wasn't easy. The other kids stared in the playground and called us names. Sweet Adu and little Bluebell eventually won them over. Adu and I grew even closer and haven't spent a single night apart. She's Craw to me, and I to her. Life for life.

Our parents found jobs, and somewhere for us all to live. Ma worked on the building sites around the city. Da got a job as a teacher. For years, Ma refused to sculpt or talk about mermaids.

Finally, we saved enough money for tickets to sail to Farland. When we arrived at the port, Elen was waiting with my family. Granma and Granda wept when they saw how big Adu and I had grown, though Bluebell was as tiny as ever.

It was a long haul, but the day came when Ma started creating mermaids and looking over the sea towards Craw. When she heard the rumour about advisors and rebuilding, she stomped into her workshop. All we heard was crash—bang—wallop.

Until Adu, Bluebell, and I led her into the sea to listen.

17

Dear listener,

My letter is at an end. I hope, and trust, our story is just beginning. That I'll meet with you soon. My family and friends survived. Each of the mermaids that left the six factories reached her destination, and so did all of the people inside.

They've started families and careers. They write regularly, of good lives and new languages. All miss Craw and would gladly return to end the curse that has gripped our city for too long. Too easily, we gave way to hate and greed that devoured our home, our cultures, and way of life.

There's more. *What of the children who were forced to fight?* The boy in our garden and the young soldiers? I like to think he deliberately aimed badly, and would have let us go.

What happened to the brave girl with the knife who saved Bluebell? The one who looked beyond war and saw an animal who needed her?

As far as I know, no records exist of their whereabouts. Their names have been erased from Crawian annuls, but never from my heart. Never!

I think about them often. Every minute. With all that I am, I hope they found a safe place. I yearn to hear their stories that are the bones of the earth. Only their words can release the rivers back into Craw and coax life back to our streets.

I can't forget my brothers and sisters. Until every child, and young person forced to take up arms has been found, Sea Mother won't allow us into her city. The curse that has gripped Craw cannot be lifted until then. It's how it is. You know it as well as I.

But there's hope! We're not alone. A letter arrived last week from a man called Jon Kraken. He offers help and knows much of the missing children of Craw. Even the darkest winter blossoms into spring, my dear listener. Can't you hear the Crawian flowers calling your name? The Sand-Daisy, and the Blue-Dancer? And what about the whispers coming from the sea? It's *her*.

Sea Mother, she shall rise.

I won't take up more of your precious time. We want to come home. Walk on Craw beach and hear our own lyrical birds. Ask for bread in the bakery and speak Crawian language. Rebuild a city with my brothers and sisters. Speak. Listen. Reflect on how we were overcome by hatred. Do better. Go on, and on. Endure, and then flourish.

And look for the fortress that Adu, Bluebell, and I built when we were girls. Fortify our walls and know to always leave a door open for those who need shelter.

That's it. The end. All of our hopeful mermaid tears are embedded into this letter. The rest is up to you. Please, hear us.

I'm not going to beg, but won't you invite us back? We'll do anything to help rebuild the city. Anything, I tell you!

I'll write to the families who escaped inside our mermaids, and ask them to assist with the work. Amongst them are engineers, plumbers, bricklayers, doctors, teachers, and children. I'll do anything, and so will they.

We're strong and resilient and can sweep streets and plant flowers. I can lay bricks and build houses as well as the best of builders. Adu and I are energetic and willing. Da can construct engines and machinery. Trish? Magician of the wind. Couldn't you use her skills?

Aln and Adu are the best seam-makers this world will ever see. They'll never drop a stitch. Their work will hold tight through the wildest and most wicked of winds.

Bluebell would help too, by welcoming back the children. She's good at licking and making friends, and she can flip on demand. What city can be rebuilt without dogs?

And Ma? What of Arker Fi, guardian, and mother, of Craw? Ma can light-up a generation with kindness, instead of ignorance. Hope in place of fear. Bring back Ma, and maybe Sea Mother will forgive us.

As I said, I won't beg—much. But, please? Won't you consider it?

You've listened well. What to do next? In our girlish speak-and-listen, the title given to people who enable the trials to go ahead is *facilitator*. What do you think about that?

I'll leave it with you, dear facilitator. Best of listeners. Our address is included. Don't let us down.

Luce Fi.

Close not thine heart,
Or dim thy voice,
Sea Mother, she shall rise

Summer 2022

*Does Luce's letter reach the leaders? What happens to the lost children of Craw? Find out in **We, Kraken**. Book two of The Volcano Chronicles, by NineStar Press and Eule Grey.*

We, Kraken

A gun; under my brother's bed.

Devora Kraken seems to have everything under control and all she could ask for. Like the neighbourhood tunnels, where she can hang out with monsters and mermaids, both. If sometimes it's not clear which is which, that's only normal—right? Anyway, Devi has plenty else to keep her busy, including a good cop, bad cop set of family members. And if all of that isn't enough, there's even a cute girl at the new school across town trying to get Devi's attention!

From the deep waters of the past, something wakes up and marches through Mainland. One terrible night, blood is spilt, and gangs gather in the woods. Devi's cousin, Jon, leaves for the speak-and-listen trials, and nothing will be the same again.

Devi sets off on a journey of discovery that will take her from her home in Exer City, across Mainland, and into Craw. It won't be easy—her brother Korl refuses to talk about the past, or why Jon left. He won't speak of the gun under the bed, or the pile of mermaid figurines. Korl refuses to talk about anything!

What's a monster anyway? Who better than Devora Kraken to find out?

Author bio

Eule Grey has settled, for now, in the UK. She's worked in education, justice, youth work, and even tried her hand at butter-spreading in a sandwich factory.

She writes novels, novellas, poetry, and a messy combination of all three. Nothing about Eule is tidy but she rocks a boogie on a Saturday night!

For now, Eule is she/her or they/them. Eule has not yet arrived at a pronoun that feels right.

The Volcano Chronicles

Book one: *I, Volcano*
I, Volcano – NineStar Press
Book 1.5: *The Flying Mermaid*
Book two: *We, Kraken*. Coming summer 2022 from NineStar Press.

I, Volcano

We pivot on a T-junction.

I'm the left arm of the *T*, tugging towards the sea, and home. Corail is the right arm, leaning towards Esk. There are no certainties. Whichever way we take could mean death. She breaks free, pushes my shoulders, and roars a guttural, inhuman noise.

"Enough! Jalob, you have to leave. Go!"

Her raw anger blasts me backwards, straight into a pile of fishing nets. In the panic to stay upright, I land badly. The pain is bad, but not from my ankle.

As if a decision has been made, she starts walking in the direction of the city. I can't take it.

"Where are you going? You haven't given me a chance to explain. Come back!"

Her head jerks to the side, but my call doesn't stop her. Without faltering, she keeps walking, and the distance between us increases.

But she's too weak for speed. I catch up easily and pull at her arm. Stress and adrenaline affect my mastery of the accent. My inadequate words are stilted and awkward. I don't convey strength, certainty, or the depth of my emotion.

"We can escape. It's still possible. My father says—"

She looks up. Moonlight illuminates the face that's always on my mind. "Nothing matters anymore." Her voice catches on too much anguish to be contained. "You have to go home, and I've got to join the army. Everything else is irrelevant."

"No." I tried to pretend it would not come to this. When she played the violin and music lifted us far from guns and soldiers, sometimes I forgot. It was me who ignored the temptations of despair and hatred, finding endless ways to cheer her up. Perhaps I was wrong. An ocean full of sea creatures can't make us forget the things we've seen. "No," I repeat, unsteadily. "That's not true."

"Our paths lead in opposite directions," she states, her voice hollow. "It's the only truth that matters."

She watches my battle to accept her destroying words and then takes my hands. "Go, Jalob. Please? Don't make this any harder than it already is. Let's just do it. Quickly! I'll walk this way, and you, that."

"I can't do that!" I wail. "Please, don't leave me."

"You ogre! Why are you making this difficult?"

She's never sworn at me before, and I've never begged. She doesn't sound like Corail, and I don't sound like Jalob. We're stifled people, squashed as flat as fruit on a concrete road.

By hunger.

Fear.

Death.

Impossible choices.

By the inevitability of today, of this moment that has slunk towards us, gathering pace. Whichever decisions we chose, we were always going to end up on this beach, caught like crabs in a fishing net.

"You're killing me. Every minute you keep me here makes it worse," she says. "There's no time left."

She's right. All the nights her head found a bed on my body and we dozed the hours away have leaked into yesterday. I want back every second. What a fool I was, to waste time sleeping!

I'm a hare caught in the headlights of her apocalypse eyes. Her name is all I can manage, and it's a cry wrenched from my vital organs. "Corail!"

"Go. Please." She pushes again, this time more of a caress than a show of force. Her head hangs low.

Our impasse ends abruptly, with deafening crashes and apocalyptic bursts of light. Each splintering blast means more ancient buildings destroyed. One heap of rubble collapses onto the next. All the arches that led from one flowering pathway to the next have been crushed. There are no options and no pathways in this city anymore.

We should be used to bombing; nevertheless, we leap into each other's arms. She dives into my body the same way a person welcomes bed on a cold night. I'm where she belongs.

"Jalob," she whispers. "I'm so scared."

Printed in Poland
by Amazon Fulfillment
Poland Sp. z o.o., Wrocław